D1101857

Where are my Shoes?

LONDON BOROUGH OF BARNET
LIBRARY SERVICES
WITHDRAWN AND OFFERED
FOR SALE
SOLD AS SEEN

PRICE	

A fantasy story
in a familiar setting

30131 05261712 0

LONDON BOROUGH OF BARNET

First published in 2003 by
Franklin Watts
338 Euston Road
London
NW1 3BH

Franklin Watts Australia
Level 17 / 207 Kent Street
Sydney
NSW 2000

Text © Karen Wallace 2003
Illustration © Deborah Allwright 2003

The rights of Karen Wallace to be identified as the author
and Deborah Allwright as the illustrator of this Work have
been asserted in accordance with the Copyright, Designs
and Patents Act, 1988.

All rights reserved. No part of this publication may be
reproduced, stored in a retrieval system, or transmitted
in any form or by any means, electronic, mechanical,
photocopy, recording or otherwise, without the prior
written permission of the copyright owner.

A CIP catalogue record for this book is available
from the British Library.

ISBN 978 0 7496 5368 2

Series Editor: Jackie Hamley
Series Advisors: Dr Barrie Wade, Dr Hilary Minns
Design: Peter Scoulding

Printed in China

Franklin Watts is a division of
Hachette Children's Books.

To Glen, from K.W.

Where are my Shoes?

Written by
Karen Wallace

Illustrated by
Deborah Allwright

FRANKLIN WATTS
LONDON•SYDNEY

Karen Wallace
"I love writing funny books so I can laugh at my own jokes. I wish I'd had a pair of shoes like Jack's when I was younger!"

Deborah Allwright
"I'm always working towards making my shoe collection even bigger!"

Jack is cross. "Where are my shoes?"

5

Are they under the bed?

8

No, but here is a wand!

Are they behind
the door?

11

No, but here is a cloak!

Are they on the table?

16

No, but here is a top hat!

"Where are your shoes?" shouts Mum.

Abracadabra!

"Here are my shoes!"
cries Jack.

22

Notes for parents and teachers

READING CORNER has been structured to provide maximum support for new readers. The stories may be used by adults for sharing with young children. Primarily, however, the stories are designed for newly independent readers, whether they are reading these books in bed at night, or in the reading corner at school or in the library.

Starting to read alone can be a daunting prospect. READING CORNER helps by providing visual support and repeating words and phrases, while making reading enjoyable. These books will develop confidence in the new reader, and encourage a love of reading that will last a lifetime!

If you are reading this book with a child, here are a few tips:

1. Make reading fun! Choose a time to read when you and the child are relaxed and have time to share the story.

2. Encourage children to reread the story, and to retell the story in their own words, using the illustrations to remind them what has happened.

3. Give praise! Remember that small mistakes need not always be corrected.

READING CORNER covers three grades of early reading ability, with three levels at each grade. Each level has a certain number of words per story, indicated by the number of bars on the spine of the book, to allow you to choose the right book for a young reader:

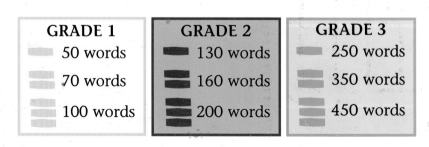

GRADE 1	GRADE 2	GRADE 3
50 words	130 words	250 words
70 words	160 words	350 words
100 words	200 words	450 words